EASY CHAPTER

THE
SMALL POTATOES
AND THE SLEEP-OVER

Harriet Ziefert and Jon Ziefert
Illustrated by Richard Brown

A Yearling Book

Published by
Dell Publishing Co., Inc.
1 Dag Hammarskjold Plaza
New York, New York 10017

Text copyright © 1985 by Harriet Ziefert

Illustrations copyright © 1985 by Richard Brown

All rights reserved. No part of this book may be reproduced
or transmitted in any form or by any means, electronic or
mechanical, including photocopying, recording, or by any
information storage and retrieval system, without the written
permission of the Publisher, except where permitted by law.

Yearling ® TM 913705, Dell Publishing Co., Inc.

ISBN: 0-440-48036-1

Printed in the United States of America
First printing—July 1985
CW

For the real camper in our family

CHAPTER ONE

MAKING PLANS

Hi. We're a group.

We have a club and a clubhouse.

We call ourselves the *Small Potatoes*.

Come on in.

There's Roger, Sam, Chris,

Molly, Sue, Scott, and Spot.

Roger wears glasses. Sam has freckles.

Chris is tall and Molly is not.

Sue has braids and Scott does not.

And Spot is Spot. (He's also Molly's dog.)
Right now we're going to have a meeting.

You can join in.

There's plenty of room.

"Can't we do something that doesn't cost
  anything?" asked Sue.
"Let's sleep over in the clubhouse,"
  shouted Sam.
"Great idea," said Sue.
"*Arf! Arf!*" barked Spot.

"What do we need for a sleep-over?" Molly asked.

"Sleeping bags."

"Flashlights."

"Food for breakfast."

"And bug spray—definitely bug spray."

"We each should bring our own sleeping bag,"
    said Roger.

"I can bring the bug spray," Sue said.

"I can bring some games," said Sam.

"Me too," said Scott.

"We don't need too many games," said Sue.
    "We can tell ghost stories."

"Should we each bring our own breakfast?"
asked Molly.

"I don't think so," answered Roger. "I
think each person should bring enough of
one thing for everybody."

"What do you mean?"

"I mean someone should bring a big box of
cereal, and someone else should bring
the milk, and someone else the bread."

"I get it," said Sam. "So let's decide
who should bring what."

Molly said, "I'll bring the milk."

Roger said, "I'll bring the juice."

Sue said, "I'll bring the cereal."

Chris said, "I'll bring the bread."

"And I'll bring a jar of peanut butter,"
    said Scott.

Spot whined.

His ears dropped and he looked very sad.

Molly knew just what was the matter.

"I'll bring food for Spot," she said.

"Bow wow," said Spot with a smile.

"Bye, everybody," said Sam. "Be back here
    with the stuff at 7:00."
"Hope it doesn't rain," said Roger as he
    rode away on his bike.
"See ya."
"See ya later."

CHAPTER TWO

THE FIRST PROBLEM

Everyone arrived with their gear.

Sam had a duffel bag.

Molly pulled a wagon.

Roger had a backpack.

Scott had a knapsack.

Chris and Sue had their stuff
strapped to their bikes.

Sue said, "First let's put down
    the sleeping bags."

Everybody agreed.

The whole group went into the clubhouse.

"Uh-oh!" said Roger. "We have a big problem.
We can't spread all six sleeping bags—
plus Spot's blanket—in this clubhouse.
We'll all be squashed!"

"Three of us will have to sleep on the porch,"
said Molly.

"Not me!" said Sam.

"Not me!" said Scott.

"Not me!" said Sue.

Spot wagged his tail.

Molly looked at her dog and said, "At least
there's one of us who will be happy
to sleep outside!"

"What's a fair way to decide who sleeps

outside and who sleeps inside?"

asked Sue.

"I know," said Chris. "We can draw sticks."

Chris found some small twigs.

He broke them so three were long and three were short.

Chris decided whoever picked the short sticks would sleep outside.

"Who's going to pick first?" Chris asked

as he held out the sticks.

Scott picked first, then everybody followed.

Scott, Molly, and Sam all got short sticks.

"It's not fair!" grumbled Sam. "There's
nothing to protect us out there!"
"Yeah!" said Scott.
"But you have Spot to protect you," said
Chris.

"*WOOF! WOOF!*" barked Spot as loud as he
could.
"I guess he's trying to show us he'll be a
good watchdog," Scott said.
"He will," said Molly.
"Hope so," said Sam as he picked up his
sleeping bag and headed for the porch.

Sam put down his striped sleeping bag.
Scott put his plaid one next to Sam's.
Spot carried his dog blanket to Molly.
She put the blanket down next to her
  sleeping bag. "Looks like
  we're all organized. Now what?"

CHAPTER THREE

EVENING ACTIVITIES

"Now we'd better spray ourselves with bug
    spray," said Roger, who definitely
    wanted to keep the mosquitoes away.
"And we'd better put the food away too,"
    said Molly. "Otherwise we might have
    bugs in our breakfast!"

"Why don't we put all the food in Molly's
     cooler?" suggested Sue.

"Good idea!"

"Enough of this getting organized!" grumbled
     Roger.

"I agree!" said Chris. "I want to have some
     fun before we go to sleep."

"What should we do?"

"Let's play Telephone," said Molly.

"Wait a minute," said Chris. "I brought my
     telescope. Doesn't anybody want to look
     at the stars?"

"I do," said Sue.

"So do I," said Sam.

Chris passed around his telescope and showed
everybody how to focus it.

"I see something big and bright," said Sue.

"It's probably Jupiter," said Chris.

When Sue gave the telescope to Roger, he
was sure he saw Mars.

"Now can we play Telephone?" asked Molly.

"How do you play?" asked Sue.

"It's easy," said Molly. "If everybody
would just sit down in a circle, I'll
show you."

"I'm going to whisper a sentence into Chris's
ear," said Molly.

"And I'm supposed to whisper it to someone
else?"

"Right!"

"So let's get going," said Scott, who was getting
impatient.

Molly started the game. She whispered:

"The Small Potatoes are the very best."

Chris heard what Molly said and passed the
sentence to Sam.

Sam passed it to Roger.

"What did you say?" asked Roger.

"No repeating!"

So Roger whispered what he heard to Sue.

And Sue whispered it to Scott.

Scott looked puzzled.

"Tell us the message!"

"Here goes," said Scott. *"Eat lots of
      potatoes, then take a rest."*

"That's not what I said!" Molly giggled.

"This is fun," said Chris. "Let's play
      one more round."

"I think we'd better get our flashlights,"
said Roger. "It's getting very dark."
"Maybe someone can think of a flashlight
game," said Sam.
"I think I know one," said Sue. "Why don't
we shine the lights on one of the blankets
and make shadows?"
"Great," said Chris. "We can experiment and
see what animal shapes we can make."

Molly said, "We'll all take turns and
the best shadow wins!"

"Let's get started," said Roger.

Roger struck a pose.

"He's a scary wolf!" cried Scott.

"Mine's a bird," said Sue.

"And mine's a cat," said Sam.

No one could guess what Molly and
Spot made together.

What do you think their shadow looks like?

When it got really late, Molly said,
    "Now it's time for ghost stories."
"Who knows a good one?" asked Roger.
"My uncle once told me a very scary
    story," said Sam.
"Let's hear it!" shouted everyone.
  So Sam began:

There once was a family—two parents,
three children—who set out together
to visit a big, old house. They climbed
stairs and ladders to get to a tower.
All of a sudden, Mother disappeared into
thin air. . . .

"I don't want to hear any more," said Sue.
    "It's too scary!"
"I don't really want to tell any more,"
    said Sam. "I'm too tired."
"I'm tired too," said Chris.

28

"So why don't we go to sleep?"
"If everybody's ready, I think that's a
          good idea," said Scott.
Roger, Sam, Chris,
Molly, Sue, Scott, and Spot—
they curled up in their sleeping bags.
It seemed as if everyone was tired
enough to fall asleep.
Good night, gang.
Sleep tight.

CHAPTER FOUR

THE SECOND PROBLEM

"Move over," Chris whispered to Roger.

"I can't," Roger answered.

"Be quiet," said Sue to both of them.
 Sue was really trying to sleep.

"I smell something funny," said Chris.

"I hear a funny noise," said Roger.

"Be quiet!" said Sue again.

Scott coughed.

Sam sneezed. *"Ah-choo!"*

Molly yawned.

Spot barked. *"Arf! Arf!"*

Scott was hot.

Sam was itchy.

Molly was tired.

Spot was wide awake.

But inside the clubhouse
Roger snored.
Chris snored.
Sue snored.
Everyone was fast asleep.

Scott said, "I'm really tired."

"Let's go to sleep," Sam said.

"That's a good idea," mumbled Molly,
    who was half-asleep already.

"Good night, everybody."

When Spot saw that Molly was asleep,
he rolled over and went to sleep too.

Scott slept.

Sam slept.

Molly slept.

Spot slept until . . .

he jumped up.

Spot trembled.

Spot cried.

Spot chased his tail.

Spot made such a fuss he woke everybody.

"What's the matter with him?" asked Sam.

"He must have had a bad dream," said Molly.

"Don't be silly! Dogs don't dream!" said Scott.

"My dog dreams," insisted Molly.

"What do you think a dog dreams about?"

"I think Spot dreamed someone was chasing
        him."

"Maybe it was a fox."

"Or maybe it was the skunk he chased
        before we went to sleep."

"Enough maybes . . . maybe we should all
        go back to sleep," Roger said.

"Spot feels better," said Molly as she
        patted his head.

"So let's go back to our sleeping bags,"
        Chris said.

Roger, Sam, Chris,

Molly, Sue, Scott, and Spot—

they curled up in their sleeping bags.

Again, good night.

Sleep tight.

It's the middle of the night.

CHAPTER FIVE

LET'S EAT

"Ruff! Ruff!"

Spot's bark woke Molly first,
    then everybody else.

"Is it really morning?" asked Sam.

"It better be," mumbled Roger.

"C'mon, sleepyheads, get up!" Sue said.

"Okay. Okay. We're awake," said Chris
    and Scott.

Everybody crawled out of their
sleeping bags.

Spot began to wag his tail.

"What does he want?" asked Scott.

"He's saying, 'Let's eat,'" answered Molly.

"Great idea!"

"I'm starved!"

"Where's the food?"

"Look at Spot," said Scott, "now he's

   cleaning up."

Spot was sniffing the ground for food.

When he found something, he quickly licked

it up.

"I think we should all help Spot clean up,"

   said Molly.

"Let's put all the trash in this plastic bag."

Spot found himself a cereal bowl and
was licking the milk from the bottom.
Molly pulled it away and shouted,
"That's enough for you!"
Spot followed Molly when she carried
the bowl to the garbage bag.
"Stop following me! You've had enough
to eat!"
"I think everything is all clean,"
said Scott.
"All clean!" Sam said as he threw the
last carton into the bag.

"What do we do with the rest of
our stuff?" asked Roger.

"I think we should take everything
home, then meet at the playground,"
said Chris.

"Good idea."

"What time should we meet?" asked Sam.

"Be there in an hour," answered Sue.

Everyone agreed to be at the entrance
to the playground at 11:00.

Molly and Spot were the last to leave.

They were both tired from the sleep-over.

Spot lay on top of the wagon.

Molly slowly pulled it away from the clubhouse.

CHAPTER SIX

WHERE'S MOLLY?

First Sam arrived.

Then came Roger.

Sue and Chris came together.

Scott came next.

The whole group waited.

Where were Molly and Spot?

At 11:20 they still were not there.

Roger said, "I'm getting tired
of waiting."

"Should we go inside and forget
about them?" asked Chris.

"I think we should," said Roger.

"But what if something happened?"
asked Sue.

"Maybe we should go to Molly's house
to find out," suggested Scott.

"I don't think we should go anywhere
but inside," said Roger. "I'm mad."

"I'm mad too," said Chris. "Molly promised
to be here."

"Who wants to race me to the top
　　of the jungle gym?" asked Roger.
"I will," answered Chris.
　And before anyone realized it, the
two of them were gone.

Scott looked at Sue.

He said, "I'll ride to Molly's house
    with you."

"I'll come too," said Sam.

"There must be a good reason why Molly
    and Spot are late," said Sue.

Sam rang the doorbell.

At first there was no answer.

Then Molly opened the door.

Spot was behind her.

They both looked funny.

"What happened to you?" asked Sue.

"We were worried," said Scott.

"Spot and I were tired when we got home,"
said Molly. "I lay down on my bed
for a rest—and I guess I fell asleep."

Molly looked at Spot. "Why didn't you wake
me up?" she asked him.

He looked confused. "I guess Spot's still
half-asleep," said Molly.

Just then there was a screech of brakes.
Roger and Chris hopped off their bikes
and ran toward the house.
"It was no fun at the playground without
      all of you," said Chris.
"And we wanted to know what happened,"
      Roger said.

"Well," said Molly, "everything's all right.
Spot and I just fell asleep."
"I'm pretty tired myself," said Chris.
"I could use a nap," said Sue.
"Me too," said Sam.
"Before everyone leaves, let's make a time
for a meeting," said Molly.
"How about tomorrow at 11:00?"
Everyone said they could come.

So tomorrow is the next meeting of
The Small Potatoes Club.

Hope you can come.

And bring your membership card.

"See you next meeting!"

SMALL POTATOES FUN

• Did you ever camp out? Tell or write the story of your very own camping adventure.

• Did anyone ever not meet you when they promised they would? What did you do?

• Since you are now a member of *The Small Potatoes Club*, make a membership card for yourself. You can copy the one below or invent your own.